YOU C

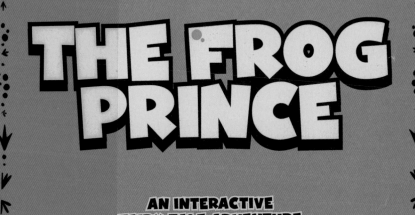

THE FROG PRINCE

AN INTERACTIVE
FAIRY TALE ADVENTURE

written by Blake Hoena
illustrated by Mariano Epelbaum

CAPSTONE PRESS
a capstone imprint

You Choose Books are published by Capstone Press, an imprint of Capstone.
1710 Roe Crest Drive
North Mankato, Minnesota 56003
www.capstonepub.com

Library of Congress Cataloging-in-Publication data is available on the Library of
Congress website.
ISBN 978-1-5435-9012-8 (library binding)
ISBN 978-1-4966-5812-8 (paperback)
ISBN 978-1-5435-9016-6 (eBook PDF)

Summary: Using a choose-your-own-format, readers navigate their way through
three twisted versions of the classic fairy tale "The Frog Prince."

Editorial Credits
Editor: Michelle Parkin; Designer: Brann Garvey; Media Researcher: Eric Gohl;
Production Specialist: Kathy McColley

All internet sites appearing in back matter were available and accurate when this book
was sent to press.

Printed and bound in the USA.
PA100

TABLE OF CONTENTS

ABOUT YOUR ADVENTURE

A land ruled by magic can be a tricky place. One wrong move, and your life could be changed forever. No one is safe—even princes and princesses can be caught under the spell. Be careful. Things are not always what they seem. Those who do not listen to the warnings have been known to croak.

In this fairy tale, you control your fate. Leap into the story and make choices to determine what happens next. Chapter One sets the scene. Then you choose which path to read. Follow the directions at the bottom of the page as you read the stories. The decisions you make will change your outcome. After you finish one path, go back and read the others for new perspectives and more adventures.

CHAPTER 1

A MAGICAL WORLD

You live in a world of make-believe. It's a land ruled by brave princesses, mighty princes, and powerful kings. All the far-away fantasy lands you have heard of exist here. Monsters and ogres roam the land. Sorcerers, witches, wizards, and fairies cast their spells across the kingdom. This is a place where magic is real.

And, since this is a kingdom, the royal family rules. In the center of the realm stands a towering castle. There, a king lives with his three daughters. The king is fair and popular among the people. The princesses are kind, but mostly stay to themselves.

In the northern part of the realm, there is a sprawling city. People travel from far and wide to see the city and buy magical goods. Invisible cloaks, flying carpets, magic wands, and cauldrons that can perform spells by themselves are popular items. There's also the Pixie Dust Spa and Resort, the Magical Amusement Park, and the Elfin Elite Club.

In the southern reaches of the kingdom is the enchanted forest. Magical creatures such as unicorns, fairies, and mermaids call this place home. Mischievous imps and goblins dwell deep in the forest. They are known for stealing the crown right off a prince or princess's head.

In this magical world, what role do you play?

To be a space princess trapped on a deserted moon,
turn to page 11.

To be a handsome prince with a green complexion,
turn to page 41.

To have an adventure in an enchanted forest,
turn to page 75.

CHAPTER 2

ROBO FROG 2000 EX

You are the space princess, Cygni—the youngest of the galactic king's three daughters. Your older sisters, Delphini and Ursa, rule your planet by your father's side. One day, the four of you decided to visit the Frog Nebula for a well-earned vacation. But on the way, your spaceship's computer went on the fritz. You crash-landed on a deserted moon.

Luckily, you ended up near a lush garden. Large fruit trees surround it. A pond of clear blue water is in the middle. You have plenty of food and water. But your father hurt his leg during the crash. He can barely move. Even worse, it may be a while before you are rescued. The ship's tracking device was damaged in the crash.

To pass the time, your father tells tales from when he was a young prince. Unfortunately you've heard them all before.

"... then the stellar dragon let loose with its fiery breath!" he says.

"Not this one again," Delphini whispers.

"... but I was not afraid," your father continues. "I raised my energy shield and drew my sword!"

"We've heard this a million times before," Ursa whispers.

Just as he was getting to the part about slaying the dragon, the king starts to COUGH! and CHOKE! and HACK!

"It's so hot and dusty," he says, clearing his throat. "Could one of you please fetch me a drink of water?"

"I will! I will!" Delphini says, eager not to have to listen to the story. She grabs a glass from the ship and takes off running toward the pond.

As you wait for Delphini's return, you hear a loud yell. She comes running back.

"What happened?" the king asks, pointing to the empty glass.

"There is a talking frog by the pond," Delphini says, scrunching up her nose in disgust. "He asked if I wanted to be his girlfriend."

Ursa rolls her eyes. "Geez, drama queen. It's just a frog." She grabs the glass and skips off to the pond.

A moment later you hear her shout, "Ugh, no!" Then she comes running back.

"What happened to the water?" the king asks, pointing to the empty glass.

"That frog asked me to marry him," Ursa says, sticking her tongue out in disgust.

"Fine, I will do it," you say with a sigh.

As you head toward the pond, you hear your father shout, "Don't forget your PPD!"

"I won't!" you yell back.

You reach into your pocket and pull out a small object. It looks like a rubber ball. The letters "PPD" are etched across it. That is short for Personal Protection Device. When activated, the ball creates a protective energy shield around the user. It can also shoot energy blasts. Every kid on your planet has one. You toss your PPD into the air and catch it before it hits the ground.

Halfway to the pond, you climb up a small hill. It provides a great view of your surroundings.

Thanks to the pond, everything nearby is green. But beyond that lies a wasteland. Sandy dunes fill the horizon.

In the distance, you spy a large metallic object glinting in the sun. It is your spaceship, *The Prince*. It is nearly covered in sand.

As you continue walking, you toss your PPD up and down, up and down. You throw it up again. But as you go to catch it, you trip over a rock. The ball hits the ground with a soft thud and rolls down the hill. Your father would be furious if you lost your PPD, so you run after it.

The PPD bounces over tree roots. It rolls under leafy plants. It does not stop until it thumps into a gigantic metal frog next to the pond.

Turn the page.

That must be the frog my sisters saw, you think.

It looks like a frog. But it is about the size of a mountain.

When you reach down to pick up your ball, you notice a big red button on the frog's underside.

"Hmmmm, I wonder what that's for?" you say out loud.

You consider pushing the button, just to see what it does. But then you remember the problems your sisters had with the frog. Maybe it would best to just grab your PPD, get the water, and leave.

17

To grab your PPD, turn to page 18.
To push the red button, turn to page 19.

You reach down to pick up your PPD, careful not to bump into the frog. But as you get closer, the frog begins to hum—as if it is booting up. Then its eyes flicker open.

"Hey!" you shout, jumping back in surprise.

"I. Am. The. Guardian. Of. The. Pond," the robot frog beeps, towering over you.

The frog is huge. It could squash you like a bug. You'd feel a lot better if you had your PPD. Maybe you could quickly grab it. Or perhaps you should call your father for help. He was just telling you about his days as a dragon slayer. Battling a frog would be a breeze after that.

18

To get your PPD, turn to page 21.

To call for your father, turn to page 23.

What harm could a little button do? you think. *It's just a frog.*

You push the red button. Something inside the robot begins to hum. Then its eyes flicker open. You jump back.

"I. Am. Robo Frog 2000 EX," it beeps. "How. Can. I. Assist. You?"

"Hello. I am Princess Cygni," you say. "And I'd like my PPD back, if you don't mind."

The frog looks down at the ball-shaped device at its feet.

"You. Can. Have. It," the robo frog beeps. "If. You. Take. Me. With. You."

Just then, you hear your father shout. "Is everything all right, Cygni? Where's my glass of water?" That is followed by a loud *COUGH!* and an even louder *CHOKE!*

You almost forgot why you came down to the pond in first place. You need to get your father some water.

"And I need a glass of water for my father," you tell the frog.

"I. Will. Give. You. Water. And. The. PPD. If. You. Take. Me. With. You," it repeats.

You consider the request. You need your PPD and the water. But this is a strange robot on a deserted moon. You don't know if it's safe to bring around your family. Maybe you can trick it.

20

To take the frog with you, turn to page 28.

To trick the frog, turn to page 30.

You are not going to be some giant frog's dinner. You need that protective shield now. Instead of calling for help, you quickly duck down and grab your PPD. Then you hold it out in front of you.

But you have never used your PPD before. You can't remember if you need to squeeze it once or twice to activate it. You give it one squeeze. Suddenly an energy blast shoots out from the ball and strikes the frog. ZZZT! Sparks flicker across the frog's metal body.

"Whoops! Sorry," you say to the frog.

OK, one squeeze for the energy blast, two squeezes for the shield, you think. Got it!

Turn the page.

You point the PPD again, ready to activate the shield.

"Wait," the frog beeps as its limbs start to twitch. "Don't. Shoot. I. Can. Help. You."

"Help me? How?" you ask.

"First. Push. Reset. Button," it beeps. "And. I. Will. Tell. You."

Pushing the button means getting close to the frog. It may be a trick to get you close enough to attack. You didn't mean to shoot it the first time, but the frog may not see it that way. On the other **22** hand, you feel bad for blasting the frog. What if it's hurt?

To push the button, turn to page 26.
To blast the frog again, turn to page 27.

Your father is a mighty king. He has slain stellar dragons and other fearsome space creatures. Yes, he was a young prince then. But surely he can get a tiny ball from a robotic frog.

"Father, help!" you shout.

Just then, the giant frog opens its mouth. A long, metallic tongue darts out. The PPD flies off the ground and sticks to the tongue.

"Hey!" you shout. "My father is not going to be very happy about that!"

Luckily, you see your father coming up the hill. He has his shield and sword. But you forgot about his injured leg. As he comes limping down the hill, he stumbles and falls.

"Oo, ow, oo!" he cries as he rolls and bounces down the hill. He doesn't stop until he hits the bottom with a crash.

BEE-OONG! The frog's tongue darts out again and grabs the king's shield. The shield disappears in the frog's mouth. The king slowly stands, holding his sword toward the frog. But the frog is ready. *BEE-OONG!* The sword—and the king—go flying into the frog's mouth too.

"No!" you scream. You turn to run. But . . . *BEE-OONG!*

The world goes black as the frog's metal mouth closes around you.

THE END

To follow another path, turn to page 9.

You feel bad you blasted the frog. You didn't mean to. You decide to help it. Cautiously, you lean over and push the red button. Suddenly, something inside the frog begins to hum and sputter.

"I. Am. Robo Frog 2000 EX," it beeps.

"Hello, Robo Frog 2000 EX. I'm Princess Cygni," you say. "I would like to get a glass of water from your pond."

"You. May," the frog beeps. "But. Only. If. You. Take. Me. With. You."

26 You are not sure what to do. You know your sisters will be angry if you bring the frog back with you. Maybe it would be better to just take the water and run.

To take the frog with you, turn to page 28.

To trick the frog, turn to page 30

You walk closer to the frog, pointing your PPD at it for protection. Suddenly the frog leaps forward and attacks!

You squeeze your PPD as hard as you can. A large energy blast hits the robotic frog. Sparks shoot all over its body. The frog starts to smoke as its internal circuits are fried.

"End. Pond. Simulation," the frog beeps.

An instant later, the pond, the trees, and the lush garden surrounding you disappear. You thought it was strange that this small patch of green existed here. Everything else is a wasteland. Now you know why—the robot frog created it.

Without the garden and the pond, you have no water, no food, and no way to survive. You and your family will starve before you can be rescued.

THE END
To follow another path, turn to page 9.

"Okay," you say. "I promise to take you with me."

"Thank. You," the frog beeps.

Then you dip the glass into the pond. When it is full, you head back to where your father and sisters await your return.

Behind you, the robotic frog hops along. *BOING! BOING! BOING!*

When you see your father, you hold out the glass and say, "Look what I brought for you!"

"Thank you," he says, taking the glass

from you.

But before the king can take a sip, your sisters both screech in horror. He drops the glass in surprise. The glass shatters at his feet.

The king begins to *CHOKE!* and *HACK!* some more.

"That's the frog. The one that wanted a date!" Delphini shrieks.

"That's the frog. The one that asked to marry me," Ursa cries. Both of them pull their PPDs out of their pockets.

You need to do something quick. Your sisters are about to attack the robo frog. And your father is in danger as well. He's sitting right in the middle of it all.

29

To save the frog, turn to page 35.
To get your father to safety, turn to page 38.

It's not safe to bring an alien frog back to the royal family. You do not know what it is capable of. But you do need your PPD back. Your father would be furious if you lost it. Those things are not cheap.

"Okay, I promise to take you with me," you lie to the frog.

You reach under the robot and pick up your PPD. But just then, you get an idea. You quickly bend down and push the red button on its underside.

"What. Are. You. . . ." the frog beeps.

The robot's eyes flicker and turn black. It worked! The robot frog is off.

You fill the glass with water and head back to where your family waits.

When you reach your father, you hand him the glass.

"Ah, thank you," he sighs as he takes a big gulp.

Afterward, you and your sisters collect fruit hanging in the nearby trees for lunch. Your father slices them up with his laser sword, and you begin to eat.

Just then, a loud *CROAK!* interrupts your lunch.

"What was that?" your father asks.

"I'll go check," you say, jumping to your feet.

It can't be the Robo Frog 2000 EX, you think. *You shut him off.*

But something is making that croaking sound.

Turn the page.

You run up the hill. From there, you can see the frog by the pond. It eyes are blinking red, and its limbs are starting to move.

"What are you doing?" you yell.

"Manual. Reset," it beeps.

Reset? you think. *Oh no you don't!* You dash down the hill and push the red button again.

"No. Wait," the robot beeps. "I. Can. Help. Yoooou. . . ." The robot turns off again.

You run back to your father and sisters.

"What was that?" your father asks.

As you pick up a fruit slice, you tell your father about the robot frog and your promise to bring him back with you.

"But I tricked it," you say proudly. "And I shut it off."

You wait for your father to tell you how impressed he is with your quick thinking. But instead, he looks disappointed.

"You made a promise," the king says sternly. "You must keep your word."

"But, Father—," you begin to say.

"No buts," your father interrupts. "Go get that frog."

Your father is right. You broke your promise. You walk down the hill toward the pond with your head down. You find the frog right where you left it. You take a deep breath and push the red button. The frog beeps. Its eyes pop open.

"I'm sorry, Robo Frog 2000 EX," you say. "It was wrong of me to trick you. Please come with me."

Turn the page.

The frog seems to smile as it follows you. It hops all the way to where your family sits.

"You didn't tell me it was a Robo Frog 2000 EX!" your father exclaims as he sees the robot.

"Is that important?" you ask.

"Of course!" your father cheers. "We can replace our computer system in our ship with that robot."

"I. Said. I. Could. Help. If. You. Took. Me. With. You," the frog beeps proudly.

34 Your father takes the robot frog to your spaceship and plugs it into the computer system. Soon *The Prince* is ready to take off. As you fly back to your planet, you're glad you kept your promise to the frog. Now everyone can go home.

THE END
To follow another path, turn to page 9.

You doubt the robot frog would hurt a fly. Okay, maybe a fly is a bad example. But you do not believe it means any harm. Although you can't say the same for your sisters.

You brought the robot frog with you. Now it's in danger. You should protect it. You toss your PPD on the ground in front of the frog. An energy shield springs up and surrounds it.

Just then, Delphini squeezes her PPD and blasts the frog. The blast bounces off the energy shield. Ursa joins the fight. She fires her PPD at the frog. Again, it bounces off the shield. They continue to shoot, but their blasts are useless. Then your sisters join forces. They shoot their lasers in the same spot. The energy shield begins to weaken.

Turn the page.

In the middle of the battle, your father shouts, "Is that a Robo Frog 2000 EX?"

You turn from your sisters. "Yes, why?"

"Stop firing!" he shouts. "You'll destroy it!"

Your sisters put down their weapons.

"We can use the frog to get home!" the king exclaims. "We can plug it into our spaceship's computer system and fix *The Prince*."

"Good thing you two didn't blast it apart," you scold your sisters.

The frog agrees to fix *The Prince* in exchange for a ride to your home planet. Soon, the ship is ready to take off.

"We've had enough excitement," your father says. "Let's go home."

THE END

To follow another path, turn to page 9.

Your father is sitting between the frog and your sisters. You worry he might get hurt. You toss your PPD at his feet. Suddenly, an energy shield surrounds him. The king is safe.

ZZZT! Delphini squeezes her PPD, shooting an energy blast at the frog. Ursa squeezes her PPD and fires a second blast. *ZZZZT!*

"Stop! Stop! I order you both to stop!" you hear your father shout. He draws his laser sword and starts to cut at the energy shield around him.

"Don't destroy that robot!" your father orders.

But it is too late. The robot frog starts to smoke and sizzle. Suddenly, it explodes with a loud *Ka-BOOM!* You and your sisters are knocked back.

"That was a Robo Frog 2000 EX," your father says with a sigh.

"So what?" your sisters say together.

"We could have turned the frog into *The Prince*," your father says, defeated. When your sisters look at him in confusion, he says, "We could have plugged it into the spaceship's computer system and used it to go home."

"Oh," you and your sisters all sigh.

Your family remains stranded on the deserted moon. You have water to drink and fruit to eat. But you have no idea when you will be rescued. It could take weeks, months, or even years . . . if anyone comes at all. It will be a long, lonely wait.

39

THE END
To follow another path, turn to page 9.

CHAPTER 3

THE POPULAR PRINCE

You are Prince Smugly, one of the most popular princes in Snooty Kingdom. You have a huge fan following online and love the attention.

Like all princes in the realm, you have a busy schedule. There is your charity work at the magical animal rescue. There are guest appearances at local events, like shooting the first arrow at the Shining Knight Games. Then there are the paparazzi, who are always following you around.

One night, you are at the grand opening of a new display at the enchanted forest. On your way out of the woods, lights flash as photographers snap your picture. Fans hold out shields for you to sign.

Your faithful bodyguard, Heinrich, guides you through the adoring crowd. You smile for the cameras, but the flashes are blinding. You try to give fans your autograph, but they are constantly shoving things in your face.

At one point, a fuzzy blue orb of light flitters in front of you. You are not sure what it is. You raise a hand to protect your eyes. You can make out a tiny face and buzzing wings. It's a fairy! But it's too late. You've already swatted at it. The soft blue light turns to an angry red.

You try to apologize for the mistake, but your voice is drowned out by excited shouts from the gathered crowd.

"It's a fairy! It's a fairy!" the people yell.

Fairies are almost as popular as princes. The paparazzi push to get closer.

"And she's angry," someone adds.

The fairy points her tiny wand directly at you. Suddenly you feel dizzy. Colorful lights swirl about. Your stomach twists and churns. Your legs grow weak, and you collapse to the ground.

One moment, you are surrounded by fans and flashing lights. The next, you are covered in a pile of clothes. You poke your head out of the mess. You call for help, but all that comes out is *CROAK!*

Turn the page.

"Prince Smugly has been turned into a frog!" someone exclaims.

The crowd gasps. Cameras flash. The next thing you know, you are being scooped up and shoved into someone's coat pocket. You hear a car door slam and the screech of tires.

"Sorry about that, your highness," Heinrich says as he pulls you out of his pocket. "But I had to get you out of there. You'd make a tasty snack for a hungry dragon or some other magical beast."

You catch your reflection in the review mirror. A big bullfrog stares back at you.

"I'm green!" you croak.

You look down at your webbed fingers. You cannot be seen like this. What will your fans say?

You sit back on your froggy legs and wonder what to do. You could seek out the fairy who did this and demand she remove the spell. Or maybe you should hide out until the spell wears off. It can't last forever, right?

To go looking for the fairy, turn to page 46.

To hide out, turn to page 49.

You are mad. If your face wasn't green, it would probably be bright red right now. You cannot live like this. You are a prince, not a frog!

"Heinrich, track down that fairy!" you order.

"On it, your highness," Heinrich replies. He tells your limo driver to head to Cauldron Alley. "We can hire a PIW, a private investigator witch," he explains. "She will hunt down the fairy for us."

The PIW is expensive, and she doesn't give you a celebrity discount. It seems as though she stares into her black cauldron for days. Eventually, though, the witch is able to see the fairy's location.

"She is a singer at the Elfin Elite Club," she tells you.

You speed to the club as fast as you can. Luckily, frogs aren't as trendy as princes. It has been much easier getting from place to place.

Heinrich barges into the club with you in his hands. You see the fairy singing up on stage.

"There you are, you wicked fairy!" you shout. "Turn me back into a prince."

"Sorry, Princey. That's not how magic works," the blue fairy says defiantly. "I cannot just turn it off. And," she adds, "I wouldn't, even if I could!"

The fairy has you at a disadvantage. You cannot do much as a frog. But you have Heinrich with you. He can force that fairy to change you back. Then again, you remember what happened the last time you made her angry. Maybe you should use your princely charm on her instead.

To force the fairy to change you back, turn to page 53.
To ask how to change back, turn to page 55.

Fairies can be mean when they want to be. You have already had one run-in. You do not want to make matters worse. The fairy could turn you into a slimy slug or worm next time.

Instead of confronting the fairy, you decide to get out of the limelight. This is probably a good time to go on a retreat. You could hit the supernatural spa, soak in a mythical mud bath, or do a little unicorn yoga.

"Heinrich, get me out of here," you say. "I need a place to hide out for a while.

Hours later, you find yourself at the Pixie Dust Spa and Resort. It is a private retreat for royalty. You spend your days sunning on a lily pad in the garden pond.

Sometime later, you are awakened by a loud splash. You hear a cry. "Oh, no! I've dropped my bracelet!"

You look up and see Princess Daisy. You've seen her before in your royal social circles. She is known for being a bit clumsy. In fact, people call her Princess Oopsy Daisy behind her back.

Right now the princess looks quite upset. You are about to ask her what is wrong. After all, it is your sworn duty as a prince to help anyone in distress. But then you remember you are not a prince anymore. How could you possibly help anyone in your current state? You watch as the princess reaches down into the water.

"It's too deep," Princess Daisy mutters to herself. "I can't reach it." She sits back on the grass.

Turn the page.

You realize you can help the princess. As a frog, you could dive down into the water and get her bracelet. But saving the day would draw attention to you. Your frog face is probably all over the internet. The last thing you want to do is risk damaging your princely image any further.

To hide from the princess, turn to page 57.

To help the princess, turn to page 59.

You may be a frog, but you're still a prince. You should not have to ask the fairy to change you back. The fairy should simply do as you command.

"Heinrich, I think it's time to show this fairy we mean business," you croak.

Your bodyguard draws his sword and slashes at the fairy. She zips to the right. Heinrich slices and misses. She darts to the left as he jabs and misses again.

After a few more attempts to slice and dice, jab and stab the fairy, she has had enough.

"I'm tired of this game," she says. "I had hoped you both would have learned a lesson from this. It looks like I was wrong."

The fairy changes from her soft blue color to a brilliant red. She waves her tiny wand. Sparkling colors start to swirl around Heinrich.

"What is happen—" he begins. "HISSS!"

"Oh, no!" you croak.

54

Your bodyguard has been turned into a huge snake! The snake stares at you hungrily.

"You devious fairy!" you curse. You try to hop away, but you are not fast enough to escape Heinrich's strike. You become a snake snack.

THE END

To follow another path, turn to page 9.

Being a frog is pretty bad, but you're sure things could be worse. You do not want to risk angering this fairy again. Instead, you turn on the princely charm.

"We got off to a bad start. I didn't mean to hurt you," you say to the fairy. "I'm so sorry I swatted you like some pest. It was an accident, and I beg your forgiveness."

The fairy softens a bit. Her blue light glows brightly.

"Thank you for your apology," the fairy says.

"Please, is there any way you can change me back to a prince?" you plead. "I promise never to harm another fairy." You add a final "please" for good measure.

"It's not what I can do," the fairy says. "To change back, you will need a princess."

"Can you be more specific?" you ask.

But just then, the doors burst open. A huge crowd pours in.

"I need to get to my dressing room," the fairy buzzes. "I am the headliner tonight."

She flutters off, leaving you and Heinrich in the middle of a growing crowd.

"Wait! How does a princess change me back?" you call. But the fairy is gone. You sigh.

"Not to worry, sire," says Heinrich. "We can find a princess."

But what will you ask her when you find her?

To ask a princess to kiss you, turn to page 60.
To ask a princess to help you, turn to page 64.

You came to this resort to keep a low profile, and that is what you plan to do. You do not want to risk any further damage to your reputation.

How many of my fans would love me as a frog? you wonder. *Not many.*

You start to feel sorry for yourself. Instead of helping the princess, you slowly lower yourself into the water. You dive under the lily pad and hide there until she leaves.

You spend the rest of your vacation hiding from everyone you see. The fairy magic never wears off. And, it turns out, the longer you stay a frog, the more you act like one. "Ribbit" starts replacing words when you speak. You discover that flies are delicious snacks. The black ones are nice and crunchy.

Turn the page.

Slowly, you forget all about your former life as a prince. By the time Heinrich comes back to the spa to get you, he cannot tell the difference between you and the other non-royal frogs.

You spend the rest of your life swimming about the pond, completely forgotten by your fans.

THE END

To follow another path, turn to page 9.

Clearly this bracelet means a lot to the princess. For the first time, being a frog is a good thing. You know you can help her.

You leap off your lily pad and dive down deep into the pond. At its muddy bottom, you see a gold bracelet. You snatch it up in your mouth and then swim back to the surface.

Princess Daisy is beyond excited when she sees you with her jewelry.

"You fetched it for me!" she squeals with joy. She picks you and the bracelet up. "Thank you! You're such a prince."

Maybe you should tell her who you really are. But would she believe you? Maybe it would be better to stay quiet. A talking frog might startle her.

To tell her you are a prince, turn to page 67.

To remain silent, turn to page 70.

Everyone has heard stories about a princess's magical kiss. It's worth a try. You just hope the stories weren't just fairy tales.

"Heinrich, I need to get a princess to kiss me," you tell your bodyguard as he scoops you up and takes you back to your limo.

"I know just the place," he says. He whispers to the limo driver. The driver dashes off and does not slow down until you reach the Magical Amusement Park.

"Why are we here?" you ask Heinrich. "I didn't tell you I wanted to ride a roller coaster. I'm looking for a princess!"

"I know, your highness," he says. "We're here because of that." He points out the car window to a kissing booth. The sign over the booth says "Princess Kisses for $10."

Heinrich carries you over to the booth and places you in front of the princess.

"Wait, you want me to kiss a frog?" the princess asks. "Gross!"

"Please," Heinrich begs. "Your kiss may turn him into a prince!"

The princess doesn't look convinced. "I need to check with my boss about this."

She pulls out her smartphone. "Hello, Fairy Godmother? Yeah, there's another frog here claiming to be a prince. What do you want me to do?"

After a short time, the princess hangs up and turns to you. "Okay, fine. But it costs double for amphibians," she says.

Turn the page.

As you are about to pucker up, you hear a buzzing about your head. Without even thinking, your tongue darts out. You snag a big, juicy fly out of the air. As you eat, there is a flash.

"Oh, no, the paparazzi!" Heinrich shouts.

Sure enough, a photographer has just caught you on camera eating a fly. There is no way the princess is going to kiss you now. You leave the park feeling defeated.

The next day, your picture has been turned into a meme. Everyone in Snooty Kingdom has seen and shared it. Your princely popularity takes a big hit. It becomes impossible for you to convince another princess to talk to you, much less kiss you. You resign yourself to being a frog for the rest of your life.

THE END
To follow another path, turn to page 9.

Everyone in Snooty Kingdom has heard stories about princesses and their magical kisses. But those were just stories. If they were real, there would be a lot fewer frogs in the world and a lot more princes.

But the blue fairy said the cure to this mess had to do with a princess. You should at least find one and ask for help.

"Heinrich, are you thinking what I'm thinking?" you ask.

"Is it time for your mud bath?" he asks.

"No . . . well, yes," you say. That gives you an idea. "Take me to the Pixie Dust Spa and Resort."

All of the princesses hang out at Pixie Dust Spa on their days off. If you need to find a princess, you are bound to find one there.

But at the spa, finding a princess is not as easy as you might think. Being a frog makes it harder to strike up a conversation. None of princesses want to talk to you. They wrinkle their noses in disgust before you can say "Croak!"

"Ew, a talking frog," one princess says. "That's *so* last season."

"Next you're going to tell me you're a prince," another laughs.

You are quickly finding out that it is not easy being green. Discouraged, you spend the next few days moping around in the spa's garden. Suddenly, a splash brings you out of your slump.

What's going on? you wonder.

You look up to see Princess Daisy. You have seen her before at social events. She has always been a bit clumsy. She is reaching into the pond.

"This pond is too deep," Princess Daisy mumbles to herself. "I think my bracelet is lost."

You feel sorry for her. You leap off your lily pad and dive down deep into the pond. At its very bottom, you see a bracelet. You grab it with your mouth and swim back to the surface.

When you pop out of the water, the princess squeals with excitement.

"You found my bracelet!" she says. She picks you and the bracelet up. "Thank you for bringing it back to me! You're such a prince."

66 News of what happened to you is probably in all of the tabloids by now. Should you tell her who you are? Maybe she can help. Will you risk it?

To tell her, go to page 67.

To remain silent, turn to page 70.

You have nothing to lose. You are already a frog. What could be worse than that?

"Actually," you say, clearing your throat. "I *am* a prince—Prince Smugly. Maybe you've heard of me?"

Princess Daisy looks at you in surprise.

"A talking frog!" she exclaims. She is so excited that she takes a step back and trips over a lounge chair. As she stumbles, you are tossed into the air.

You land on the ground with a *SMACK!*

"Ow," you grumble.

"Oh, no, are you hurt?" the princess cries.

As she bends over to pick you up, a single tear rolls down her cheek. It falls on you. When you open your eyes, you feel different.

"You *are* a prince!" the princess shouts.

Both you and Daisy are stunned. How did this happen? As the princess helps you to your feet, a blue light flashes in front of you. It is the fairy.

"Now you know how it feels to get smacked," she laughs. "My spell has been broken." Then the fairy disappears.

"Fairy magic is a bit odd," the princess says.

"I know," you say. "I thought I would need a princess's kiss to change back."

69

Daisy scrunches up her face in disgust. "Sorry, but I would never—fly breath, you know."

You're happy to be yourself again. And you've learned a valuable lesson about swatting at fairies.

THE END
To follow another path, turn to page 9.

Not one princess has offered to help you since you got here. Why would this one be any different? You decide to keep quiet.

"You are such a great little frog," Princess Daisy says, swooping you up in her hands. "I'm going to take you home with me. My little sister would love a new pet."

Later that night, you find yourself in a terrarium. Princess Daisy's little sister keeps shoving flies in your face. You wonder if you should say something. You're not a frog, and you are certainly not a pet.

This goes on for another two days and two nights. Then on the morning of the fourth day, you start feeling a little strange. Your fingers aren't webbed anymore. Your skin isn't green. The terrarium is really cramped. You're a prince again!

You try to move. The young princess sees you, and screams. "There's a prince in my terrarium!"

Princess Daisy rushes into the room. "Hey, I know you," she says. "You're that prince that got turned into a frog for hitting a fairy."

She helps you out. You tell her the whole story. When your tale is done, a blue light flashes in the room.

"Look out! It's the fairy," you say covering your face. "Don't turn me into a frog again!"

The fairy stops in front of you. Then she looks at the princess.

"My spell has been broken," she says.

"But how? I didn't kiss him," the princess says, confused.

"That never works," the fairy laughs. "That is just a trick frogs use to get princesses to kiss them."

"I knew it!" Princess Daisy exclaims.

"The spell was broken because you were kind enough to let a slimy frog stay with you for three days and three nights," the fairy explains.

The fairy turns to leave. "And Prince Smugly, be careful who you swat at next time."

You are back to being a prince again, and you have made a new friend. The only one who is sad is Princess Daisy's little sister. She wants her pet frog back.

THE END
To follow another path, turn to page 9.

CHAPTER 4

FRIEND OR FOE

The enchanted forest is an amazing place filled with all sorts of strange creatures. You just need to know where to look to find them.

If you spot a clump of polka-dotted mushrooms sprouting from the ground, look underneath their caps. You may notice a tiny door at the mushroom's base. Most of the toadstools here aren't toadstools at all. They're homes for gnomes.

Sometimes if you stay very still, you can spot a unicorn darting between the trees. Other times, you may peek through reeds and see mermaids splashing in a pond. You've even come across dragons, elves, and goblins in this enchanted forest.

But you haven't seen any of these magical creatures today. They are all hiding, and you know why. An angry prince is stomping through the woods and making all kinds of noise.

"Where are you, you imp?" the prince shouts, holding his sword above his head. "I want my crown back."

An adventure is brewing, and you're itching to join. How will you jump in?

76

To be the prince's trusted friend, go to page 77.
To be the prince's enemy, turn to page 81.

Your name is Heinrich. You have been a faithful servant to the royal family for years. You are also good friends with the king and queen's oldest son, Prince Yellsalot. The prince hates magical creatures. He usually stays in his castle, where there are no imps, elves, mermaids, or ogres to bother him.

You are surprised to see—and hear—him charging through the enchanted forest. You chase after him.

"Your highness!" you call out and wave. "Wait, Prince Yellsalot!"

You worry about the prince's safety. He is wielding his sword. The creatures in the enchanted forest do not take kindly to people threatening them. But the prince does not hear you. He just keeps stomping through the woods.

Turn the page.

When you finally catch up to the prince, you see him waving frantically. He is trying to swat a fuzzy blue light flitting around his head.

"Hold still, you pesky pest!" he shouts.

"Your highness, stop!" you shout to the prince. "That's not a pest at all, but a fairy."

Fairies can be dangerous. They can cause all sorts of trouble with their magical spells. It's best not swat at them like they are mosquitoes.

But your warning comes too late. There is a *TINK!* as the side of the prince's sword connects with the fairy. The fairy goes flying into a tree trunk with a *THUNK!*

You can tell the fairy is furious. She turns from a soft blue to an angry red. She flies right to the prince's face and points her wand. Flashing lights swirl around him.

The prince's cry starts with, "What's happen—" and ends with a *CROAK!*

By the time you reach the prince, he is no longer a prince. His skin is green. His hands are webbed. He's shrunk to the size of your fist. The fairy has turned Prince Yellsalot into a frog!

"Oh, no!" you cry out. "This is not good. What will the king and queen think?"

The prince's sword lies next to the frog. You could use it to force the fairy to change the frog back into a prince. Or you could grab the frog and run to safety.

80

To confront the fairy, turn to page 84.
To run from the fairy, turn to page 86.

You are a blue fairy and protector of the enchanted forest. The prince stomping through the woods, waving his sword around, makes you upset. He could cut down an enchanted tree or harm the magical animals living here. You know he hates anything magical. You buzz over and get right in the prince's face.

"Stop!" you say. "How dare you bring a sword into my forest."

"An imp snuck into my castle," the prince says, shaking his sword. "He stole my crown, and I want it back. Now!"

"You don't need a sword for that," you say, trying to calm the angry prince. "Just ask nicely. Maybe tell him a joke. Imps love puns. Puns make them feel IMPortant." You laugh at your own joke.

But the prince does not find it funny or punny. Instead, he starts to wave his sword wildly in your direction.

"Hey, watch it!" you yell. "You almost hit me!"

He continues to wave his sword. He is trying to hit you! You dart out of the way, but suddenly, *TWACK!* You go flying into a tree with a *THUD!* Now you are angry. Your normally calm blue glow turns to a fiery red.

The prince will pay for striking you. A spell will teach him a lesson. But what should it be? He wouldn't be so tough as a puddle of sludge. Or maybe you should turn him into one of the enchanted creatures he hates so much.

To turn the prince into sludge, turn to page 87.
To turn the prince into a talking frog, turn to page 90.

The fairy has to change the prince back. You pick up the sword and wave it in front of you.

"What did you do to my friend?" you shout at the fairy. "Change him back this instant!"

The fairy starts to laugh. "I hope your friend likes the taste of flies. I'll never change him back!"

You feel rage growing inside you. The fairy will pay for what she did to the prince. You slice at her with the sword. She darts to your left, and then to your right.

"Hold still!" you shout. It's hard to fight

with a sword in one hand and a frog prince in the other.

The fairy shoots up and then zigzags down. You jab at her and miss again.

"Stop moving!" you snap.

The fairy stops right in front of you. You raise the sword above your head to strike. But before you can do anything, colorful lights swirl around you. You begin to feel dizzy, and your stomach twists and churns. Your legs and arms shrink.

"Hey, what's happ—" you start. "*BUZZZZZ!*" you end.

Before you can get your bearings, a long, sticky tongue hits you. *TWACK!* It pulls you in. The last thing you see is the prince's gaping mouth. You've become a crunchy fly snack for your froggy friend.

THE END
To follow another path, turn to page 9.

You saw what the fairy did to the prince when he struck her. Who knows what she would do to you. Violence got the prince into this mess. You doubt it will save him. You pick up the frog and run away as fast as you can.

"I hope you know a princess to change him back," the fairy cackles before she disappears.

You do not stop running until you are out of the enchanted forest. As you catch your breath, you try to remember what the fairy said. Something about a princess changing the prince back. But how? Do you simply give the frog to a

86 princess? You've heard stories about the power of a princess's kiss. Maybe that will break the curse.

To give the frog to a princess, turn to page 92.
To ask a princess to kiss the frog, turn to page 100.

You can think of no better revenge than to turn the mighty prince into a puddle of sludge. As a gloopy mess of goo, he will not be able harm you or anything else living in the enchanted forest. You point your wand and speak the magic words.

"Oh, prince of mine," you chant. "Today you become a puddle of slime."

Lights flash out of your wand and swirl around the prince. You watch as his head and limbs begin to shrink and shrivel. Then suddenly, *PLOP!* He falls to the ground. All that's left of the prince is a sword, a pair of boots, and some clothes in a puddle of goo.

Turn the page.

Rumors of what you did quickly spread to the prince's father. The king is furious. As a puddle of goo, the prince is slightly more useless than before. He can't go on quests or fight ogre attacks. He just sits there and oozes all over the king's furniture.

As punishment, the king removes you as the protector of the enchanted forest. You have to leave the forest at once. You try to protest but he threatens to cut down every single tree in the kingdom.

You do not wish any harm to come to your beloved home or the animals who live there. So you go. You wish you hadn't cast that spell on the prince. Yes, he needed to be taught a lesson. And he is much friendlier now as a puddle of sludge. But the king didn't find it so funny. Now you are a fairy without an enchanted home. Life is quite lonely.

89

THE END
To follow another path, turn to page 9.

Turning the prince into a magical creature sounds like the perfect revenge. You raise your arms and speak the magic words.

"Oh, prince, you did me wrong," you chant. "So I turn you into a talking frog."

Sparks fly and the smell of magic fills the air. First the prince's skin turns green. Then his arms and legs start to shrink. His buggy eyes look at you in fear as he shrinks under a pile of clothes.

You happily watch as a frog pokes its head out of the prince's royal clothes. You buzz over to him and laugh as he tries to hop. This is great fun. He will spend his days living in the forest he hates.

Just as you are about to fly off, a long tongue darts out at you. The frog captured you! You are able to get free, but it's tough.

As you struggle to catch your breath, you realize that you may not have thought this spell through. You don't want the prince eating the fairies in your forest. You have to change him back. But how? You've never had to reverse your spells before.

Princesses . . . princesses . . . something about princesses, you think.

You have heard that princesses have powerful magic. One of them could reverse the spell. But what does she have to do again? You rack your brain. Maybe he has to make a princess laugh. That could work. Or maybe she to take him home for a few days? You can't remember. You wish you paid more attention in fairy school.

To make a princess laugh, turn to page 96.

To have a princess take the frog home, turn to page 98.

Maybe if you leave the frog prince where a princess might find him, you'll get lucky. The king in the next kingdom over has a daughter. Stuffing the frog into your pocket, you rush off.

You finally reach the neighboring castle. There, you spy the princess in the royal garden. She stands next to a pond, looking down into the water.

You quietly sneak up behind her and set the frog on the ground. Then you hide behind a tree and watch. The frog hops over to the princess. She glances down at him.

"I wish you could help me," she says, sadly.

That gives you an idea.

"Maybe I *can* help. What's wrong?" you croak from behind the tree, pretending to be the frog.

The princess falls for your trick.

"I've dropped my toy ball into the water," she says, pointing to the pond. "The water is too deep for me to retrieve it. Will you be a dear and get it for me?"

"Of course, Princess," you say in the frog's voice. "But only if you promise to take me home with you."

The princess thinks for a moment, and then says, "Okay, I promise."

The frog prince seems to understand what you've said. He dives into the water. A moment later, he leaps out of the pond carrying a golden ball. The princess squeals with joy. She grabs the ball and runs off—without the frog.

"What happened?" you ask the prince. He just croaks back.

What a rude princess, you think.

Maybe you should bring the frog to the princess and remind her of her promise. But there are other princesses in the kingdom. You could find another, more honest, princess instead.

To find another princess, turn to page 100.
To bring the frog to the castle, turn to page 103.

The prince needs to get a sense of humor. Your IMPerfect joke was hilarious.

You tell him, "If you can make a princess laugh, you will change back." You smile. "Good luck with that."

The frog sticks his tongue out at you. He hops away.

Weeks later, you find the frog prince sitting on a lily pad in the middle of a pond. He is shouting at every princess who walks by.

"Did you hear the one about the sick frog?" he says. "It croaked!"

A princess rolls her eyes. "I hate coming to this garden now."

"Yeah, me too," another princess says. "You can't enjoy the flowers with that loud-mouthed frog and his terrible jokes."

"Wait. Wait. I've got a million of them," the frog says. "What's a frog's favorite kind of music?"

"I've heard this one a million times," the princess sighs.

"Hip-hop!" the frog shouts. Everyone groans.

You sit and listen to a few more bad jokes. None of them make you laugh—or even chuckle. You are quite pleased with yourself. By time the prince is able to tell a funny joke, you doubt he will ever want to come back to the enchanted forest again.

97

THE END
To follow another path, turn to page 9.

People always tell stories about magical kisses. But they are just stories. Who would actually want to kiss a frog? You certainly wouldn't.

"You will be able to change back into a prince," you tell the frog. "But only if you can get a princess to let you stay in her castle for three nights."

Days later, you spy the frog sitting near a garden pond. He is talking to a princess.

"I will retrieve your ball if you take me home with you," the frog says.

The princess agrees. "I promise."

You watch as the frog dives into the pond. When he comes back out, he is carrying a ball.

The princess quickly grabs her ball and happily runs off. She forgets all about the frog.

That's not fair, you think.

You buzz over to the sad-looking frog prince. "I'll take you to the princess's castle," you say. "She won't forget about you that easily."

It's a long flight, and the frog is heavy. You set the frog on a windowsill outside the princess's room.

"If she doesn't let you in, maybe I'll turn her into a toad," you grumble.

The frog taps on the window. Moments later, it opens. The princess peeks out and sees the frog. She hesitates but eventually picks him up and brings him inside.

The frog will change back into a prince after a few days. Hopefully, he has learned his lesson and will stay out of the enchanted forest. If not, you'll turn him into a slug next time.

THE END
To follow another path, turn to page 9.

You recall hearing stories of fairies and their magic when you were a child. In them, a princess's kiss always broke the fairy's spell. You never figured out just what was so special about a princess's kiss.

No matter. You'll have to think about that some other time. Right now you have to change the frog prince back into a prince prince. Getting a princess to kiss him is your only chance.

The best place to find a princess is at a palace. Luckily, there are plenty of those nearby. You know of a king not far away who has three daughters. Hopefully one of them will help you out.

You find the three princesses sitting around a pool in their royal garden. You approach them holding out the frog in front of you.

"Hello, your majesties," you say. "I'm Heinrich, a royal servant to the kingdom near the enchanted forest. I have something for you."

"Ew, a frog!" the eldest princess shrieks.

"No, no, it's not just any frog," you insist. "It is a prince. A human prince."

"Is this a joke?" the middle princess asks.

"You just need to kiss him one time," you say. "He'll turn back into a prince if you do."

"We're not falling for that one," the youngest princess frowns.

"Not again," the middle princess says.

"Not ever," the eldest princess adds.

Turn the page.

Before you can say anything else, the youngest princess knocks the frog out of your hands. It lands on the ground and hop, hop, hops away. You chase after him, but you are not quick enough. The frog jumps into a pond with a *SPLASH!* He dives deep under the water and disappears.

You failed to save your friend. Now you will never see him again.

THE END
To follow another path, turn to page 9.

The princess gave her word, and then broke it.

"If she won't bring you to the castle, I will," you tell the frog.

You head off in the direction that the princess ran. When you arrive at the castle, you set the frog down in front of the door. Then you knock and hide.

A moment later, the door creaks open. The king peeks out and sees the frog.

"What is a frog doing on my doorstep?" he asks.

"I am here to see the princess," you say in the frog's voice. "She promised to take me home with her after I retrieved her ball from the pond."

Turn the page.

"My daughter has never been good at keeping promises," the king says with a sigh. "It's about time she learns."

The king bends down and picks up the frog. Then he brings it inside. You climb up the castle wall to see what happens next.

"You have a visitor, my dear," the king says to the princess. "He says you have a promise to keep."

"Oh, Father," the princess whines. "It's just a frog."

You hear the king lecturing his daughter about honesty as they walk deeper into the castle. Soon you can't hear or see them anymore.

You have done the best you can do. Hopefully the princess can break the fairy's cruel spell.

Three days later, there is a knock at your door. To your surprise, you see Prince Yellsalot standing before you. He is no longer a frog. It seems that after three nights in the princess's house, the fairy's spell was broken. He and the princess are now engaged. You are generously rewarded for your service to the royal family.

THE END

To follow another path, turn to page 9.

CHAPTER 5

THE MORAL OF THE STORY

The story of "The Frog Prince" started as a folktale hundreds of years ago. It was passed down from one generation to the next. Over time, the story changed as it was told over and over again. Because of this, "The Frog Prince" has many versions. In some, the king is a merchant or a farmer. In others, the king is replaced with a queen.

One of the best known versions of this story is "The Frog King, or Iron Heinrich," by the Brothers Grimm.

In this tale, the prince is turned into a frog by a wicked witch or mean-spirited fairy. One day, the frog prince sees a princess drop her toy ball in the water. The water is too deep for her to get the ball herself. The frog prince tells her he will retrieve the ball if the princess takes him home with her. The princess agrees.

The frog dives into the spring and gets the ball. The princess is so happy to have her toy back, she runs home. She forgets all about the frog and her promise.

The next evening as she is eating dinner
with her father, there is a knock at the door. The princess opens the door and sees the frog. Frightened, she slams the door shut and goes back to dinner.

The princess's father, the king, tells her that she cannot break her promise to the frog. She lets the frog in. The frog eats at the dinner table and is given a place to sleep that night. This happens for three nights. After the third night, the princess wakes in the morning and finds a prince.

Disney's *The Princess and the Frog* is a recent version of this tale. The movie was released in 2009. In the film, the princess is a girl named Tiana. The prince is turned into a frog by a magician.

No matter the version, "The Frog Prince" teaches readers a valuable lesson—it's important to keep your word. In this story, the princess is rewarded for keeping her promise. The frog turns back into a prince and they live happily ever after.

OTHER PATHS TO EXPLORE

1. In the original fairy tale, readers never find out why the prince was turned into a frog. Can you think of some reasons why the fairy would turn the prince into a frog?

2. In chapter 4, Heinrich and the fairy are the main characters in the fairy tale. How are the stories different? How are they similar?

3. Create your own version of "The Frog Prince." Where does your story take place? How would the story change from the original fairy tale?

READ MORE

Doeden, Matt. *Beauty and the Beast: An Interactive Fairy Tale Adventure*. North Mankato, MN: Capstone Press, 2018.

Mlynowski, Sarah. *Once Upon a Frog*. New York: Scholastic Press, 2016.

Morrison, Megan. *Transformed: The Perils of the Frog Prince*. New York: Arthur A. Levine Books, 2019.

INTERNET SITES

The Frog Prince
https://www.worldoftales.com/fairy_tales/Brothers_Grimm/Grimm_fairy_stories/The_Frog_Prince.html

The Frog Prince or Iron Heinrich
https://www.pitt.edu/~dash/grimm001.html

LOOK FOR OTHER BOOKS IN THIS SERIES: